I0537673

TORN BETWEEN TWO BROTHERS

VOLUME II

(2014 Print Edition)

by

Monique Farrow

Cover Design by: Dzine18

Published by: E-Ink It

Chapter 1

Darius

"Fuck!" I roared into the exhaust filled sky. Eddie blackmailed me, after everything I did for his punk ass. My business paid for his house, his car, his wife, and his bitch. Plus all his kids, known and unknown, and the muthafucker still turned his back on me. My life wouldn't be a mess right now, if he stuck to the plan. It didn't even matter though, everything was already done.

Stealing papers wasn't as easy as it sounded. The cash came so fast, it had me thinking I was invincible, and completely off the radar. In a lot of ways, white collar crime was higher risk than hustling on the street. Even the best operation was like a house of cards. One wrong move, and the house came falling down.

I thought, I had the perfect business plan. Eddie stole the facts. Tool opened the credit accounts. And I pulled the strings from behind the scene, of course. When things went sour, I had to think fast. Eddie wasn't cooperating. Tool was clueless. And my Pops failed me in the end. I was really counting on that life insurance money, too. Too bad he fucked me over, even in death. I couldn't believe the muthafucker had the audacity to leave me a bible. If he wasn't already dead, I would've killed his ass for disrespecting me like that, and in front of a lawyer no less. Just thinking about that shit, pissed me off. I had a reputation to protect.

Unfortunately, circumstances forced my hand, literally and figuratively. In one full swoop, Tool used a red hot blade to chop it off. I was so spun, and out of my mind, I took the blade from his ass, and sliced his head off. Taking Tool out wasn't originally apart of my plan. Getting fucked up on bath salts was supposed to help me man up. So he could do his business, without me punking out. He warned me against taking that shit. But I needed something to fuck my mind up. Otherwise, I couldn't go through with it. Coke and Crystal had been good to me in the past. But, they didn't have the edge I needed go through with it. So I took the bath salts, anyway.

My house was supposed to burn to the ground with my hand inside. It was supposed to be the evidence of my death. Now that I thought about it, the original plan was stupid, and faulty as fuck. I needed a body. Thank god, Tool and I had the same build. It was his body burning up in flames, not mine. I made sure to set him aflame first. Most of his body was ash by the time I threw my hand in the fire. Everything worked out better than I planned. Damn, I could be so resourceful. I couldn't help patting myself on the back. Talk about turning lemons into lemonade. It may sound extreme, but now I was free to do whatever I wanted, without worrying about getting caught. I still had unfinished business with Eddie though. He destroyed my relationship, house, and killed my best friend, Tool. I'd have to deal with his punk ass later. Right now, none of that mattered. I had more important things to attend to like Fatima and Darius.

I didn't understand how everything went so wrong. All I needed was her cooperation. And we'd be living large right now. She'd have the house, baby, and marriage she always wanted. If she could have just held on for a little bit longer. But no. The bitch couldn't hang. On second thought, let me take that back. Fatima wasn't a bitch. She was special. I knew she wasn't cut out for the job, but I tried to bring her along, anyway. I should of asked that bitch Tasha to put in the work. She would have fucked my brother and stole his money, without a second thought. She maybe a low budget bitch, but she was a top notch ho. I had to plan better next time.

I thought Fatima could help me stay out of jail by conning my brother. The bitch hadn't got any pussy since his wife and kid died. It should have been an easy job. Looking back, I realize I was selfish, because Fatima was too delicate for a nigga like me. She was a fucking school teacher for goodness sake. I loved her so much, because she gave me a chance, anyway. Unlike everyone else in my life, she didn't judge me according to my past. I lied in the beginning of our relationship about my job, but when she found out, she stayed. When I told her about what happened to Eddie, I knew she'd leave me. But to my surprise, she didn't.

It was true, I left out the fact, I tied him to the railroad tracks. I just wanted to see what would happen. It was innocent child's play. He begged and cried. He even pissed his pants. I tried my best not to laugh, but I couldn't help it. Watching him plead for his life made me fell like a god. I got lost in the thrill, and forgot about my plan to untie him, before the train came. It really was my intention to set him free, but his cries were like cake. I couldn't eat enough. By the time, I snapped out of my trance, the train already got him. I felt bad. But what could I do. The damage was literally already done. So I walked home, and went to bed.

I trudged down the shoulder of the highway while people stuck their heads out the window laughing, cat calling, and telling me to get dressed. I had on a wife beater, pair of Calvin Klein boxer briefs, and a pair of combat boots. I had to ditch all my high tech gear after that bitch sent me flying out the window. Man I hated his guts. Ever since he were kids, Marcus was outshining or destroying my plans. Everybody preferred him. My mom. My dad.

Eddie. Childhood girlfriends. And now Fatima. I couldn't wait to take my throne back. He wasn't going to get away with breaking up my family. Fatima was going to come home, whether she liked it or not.

A red Jeep Cherokee pulled onto the shoulder, and rolled along side me. "Excuse me sir, do you need help?"

The woman driving looked well taken care of. She was an all American nip-tuck-it. The first thing I noticed was her large enhancements. Then, I scoped out the huge rock on her ring finger. She was probably an unsatisfied housewife. The look in her eyes told me she was looking for some wild Mandingo which was a good thing, because I could definitely deliver. I searched for kids in the car, but there wasn't any. She was alone. I knew she had some though, because she had a stick figure family plastered on the car window. I wanted to know how bad she wanted Mr. Johnson. So I kept walking, as if I didn't see her.

"Sir. Is everything okay?"

Bingo. I had her. As expected. She rolled with me for awhile. Then, I purposely flashed my missing hand. I figured, I might as well take advantage of my new disability.

"Oh my god.," she clutched her chest, and gasped. The look on her face was priceless. If only

5

she knew, how it happened. She looked horrified. She stopped. Jumped out of the vehicle, and ran to my side. God was good. He sent me good Samaritan at the perfect time.

"Let me see. Are you hurt?" She turned my shoulders and surveyed my body. Who knew the blows Marcus dealt would actually help me. He didn't do a lot of damage. But, the fall out the window had me dented in a few places.

"You poor thing, what happened?" She said, starring at me with crystal blue eyes.

"I got robbed a few miles back. They stole everything. My wallet, keys, and clothes are all gone." I lied. I knew it didn't matter what I said. She wanted to be my white savior, and I was more than happy to let her.

"Come here." She said, leading me to the car. And just like that, I was back in the game.

*****

I was impressed, when we pulled into the driveway. She was laid. All the houses in the addition were at least 14,000 square feet. There had to be money, clothes, a cell phone, and other things I needed inside. Getting equipped was my first step. Finding a way to meet up with Tasha was the next.

At first, I thought it would be tricky getting her to take me home. But it wasn't. I told her some sob story about being a youth minster at a local church. I said a group of young men straight out of juvenile hall took advantage of my kindness, and stole everything, including my car. Painting myself as victim, when I'm bigger than most wide receivers was a stretch, but I couldn't think of a better story at the time. I'm sure my hand gave me a little more credibility. She gave me the side eye when I was trying to fill up wholes in my story, though. She even asked, if I was lying. Instead of answering, I pulled out my dick, and she quickly shut up, and lead me inside.

"Ooh yes, it taste so good," she moaned in between strokes and blows.

Emily was gobbling me up like I was a fountain, and she was dying of thirst. I was getting the best head I had in years. Tasha couldn't even out do her, and that was saying something. My day was obviously going nowhere but up. As far as I was concerned, there was no better time to be a black man in America.

"No hands." I said, throwing her arms to the side.

Her head was banging against the kitchen cabinets, hard. But I didn't let up. I was treating her like the whore she was. The more I slammed against the back of her throat, the louder she moaned. This bitch was definitely a freak. I pulled out. Flipped her over. And fucked her from the behind.

"Who's pussy is this?" I roared.

"Yours. Daddy. Yours." She cried out in pleasure.

"Wrong answer." I pulled her across my lap, and fucked her while standing up. Her long fingernails drug across the length of my back. My skin stung as it was breaking.

"Say my name bitch. Who's pussy is this?" I demanded, pumping away.

"Ooh Marcus! It's your pussy. It's your pussy. Marcus"

Did this bitch just call me Marcus? I let go, and she went crashing onto the floor. I couldn't believe it. He fucked her too. How did he know I was even here? I darted around the kitchen, looking for his ass. He wouldn't get away from me this time. Her stark white kitchen started spinning around me. I couldn't get her voice out of my head. "It's your pussy Marcus," kept playing over, and over again in my head. Did Fatima call out his name when they were fucking too? I bet she did. I pictured myself, punishing her for breaking up our happy family, and running away. This bitch betrayed me too. And I just met her. I wasn't going to forgive her.

"What's the matter baby?" She asked, kissing and rubbing my shoulder.

What do I look like? A fucking fool. She looked up at me, innocently, like I would forget what she said. She could bat her lashes, all she wanted. But I knew the truth. And she did too. I wasn't even going to justify her question with an answer. What's the matter? She knew exactly what she did. I'm tired of having to deal with unfaithful bitches. I bet she thinks I'm going to show her mercy, but I can't. Fatima used it all, already. I gave the bitch an inch, and she took a mile. I'll never make that mistake again. This bitch fucked my brother, and had the audacity to call out his name while I was still in the pussy. Oh yes. She was going to pay.

I swag her around by her elbow. And she laughed. Obviously she thought this was a game. So why shouldn't I play along? I entered her from behind, and pulled her hair. Her oohs and aahs bounced off the kitchen walls. Until, I felt her tighten up to ride the wave. I locked my arm around her neck, just before she climaxed. I held onto my wrist with my good arm, until she no longer struggled. Then, I exploded. Today was definitely going to be a great day.

Chapter 2

Marcus

Police charged through the front door. All of them stood in the middle of my living room with guns and attitudes, ready to fire. Sadly, they just missed the horror that took place, only a few hours ago. Neither of us moved, or said a word. Even though they arrived, we were too exhausted to care. Fatima was curled up on the couch. And I was reclined in my chair.

She looked so broken and disconnected. I was starting to get concerned. We hadn't made eye contact since last night. There was no conversation, or checking of notes. Her pride was too far in the way to let that happen. I tried to wrap my arms around her, but she pushed me away. She made it clear she didn't want to talk, or be comforted. There was nothing I could do to reassure her.

I was so full of angry and rage. I wanted to rip through everything in sight. As her man, it was my job to keep her safe. And I failed. I stayed single after Allison and Jamie died for exactly this reason. I should have protected them. Why wasn't I in the car? If I was driving, things could have ended differently. Maybe they would still been alive, and last night would have never happened.

Either way, I wanted to keep my distance from Fatima to protect her from my bad luck. For whatever reason, those closest to me died. I didn't want that to happen to her. But she was so beautiful and persistent, I couldn't resist her love. It killed me to know, I was the cause of her pain. I brought the boogie man from under her bed. I should have warned her about my past, and sadistic brother. Even though, the media reported him as dead. Deep down, I knew better. The devil could die that easy. All I could do was thank god she was alive, because most people couldn't survive the hell Darius put her through. She had nothing, but my full respect. How she managed to make it while I was incapacitated downstairs, I'll never understand. I couldn't count the times, I came toe to toe with my older brother. I swear next time would be the last though, because one of us was going to die.

If it wasn't for my medical training, last night it would have been me. I fought that bastard with everything I had, but it wasn't enough. He came equipped, and well prepared. I saw nothing but blackness in front of me. But I kept throwing blows. Each time, my fist met steel. Or at least that was what it felt like. I kept alternating my shots. But all of them hit the same thing. It could have been some other defensive material. I didn't know what he was wearing. All I knew was, I couldn't get ahead. My eyes were swelled shut, early in the fight. I was literally swinging from the hip. It didn't take long before I was exhausted, and he had the upper hand. A few left hooks and upper cuts later, he had me on my knees gasping for air. Before I knew it, he was holding my head back, and running a clean blade across my throat. My own brother left me for dead. I knew he was going to find Fatima upstairs, and I couldn't let that happen, but I was fading quick. Then, I remembered there was a first aid kit in one of the bottom kitchen drawers, I just had to find it. I took of my shirt and held it against my neck while feeling my way around the kitchen. Eventually, I found my med pack. I was able to fashion a tourniquet. It stopped the blood from spilling out of my severed jugular vein. It wasn't easy, but I managed to get the job done.

When I was wrapping my neck, I could hear Fatima struggling. I feared she'd be dead, by the time I made it upstairs. Still, I couldn't give up because I could hear her crying. As crazy as it sounds, her uncontrollable sobs and intense wailing gave me strength. I knew if I could hear her voice, she was still alive. On my hands and knees, I drug myself across the living room floor. My body felt so heavy and weak, I questioned my ability to make it to her in time. I felt like passing out, every part of me wanted to lay down and die. But then god showed up. The early morning sun shown through my floor length windows. Call me crazy, but I swear I heard god telling me to get up. So I pulled myself off the ground, and limped up the long staircase.

By the time I reached the second floor I was drained. Even still, I opened the door. To my horror, I saw Satan himself. Darius was tearing into her like some beast from the underworld. Hot streams were pouring down the sides of her eyes, and she wasn't moving or saying anything. It was obvious she was there in body, but not spirit. Rage consumed me. How could I let her down? It was my job to protect her, but I failed to protect her. Just like I did Eddie, Allison, and Jamie. Out of nowhere, an inner strength took over my body. All of sudden I wasn't in pain. I was revved, and ready to go. I charged towards him with everything I had. I sent his ass flying through the two story window like a high powered missile. I prayed for his death, like I'd done several times before. Fatima rushed over and tried to check my wounds, but I wasn't there. The only thing I could see was his demise. Rushing over to the window, I hoped to see his corpse laying in the driveway, but he wasn't there. She peered over my shoulder, and looked down too. I knew she was hoping to see the same thing. When she realized he was gone, she collapsed into a bucket of tears.

We weren't able to call the police immediately. The sadistic bastard planned ahead. I had to get my home phone back online. As soon as I realized Darius was gone. I went outside, flipped the breaker box, and reset the modem in order to call the police. I knew his trail would be ice cold by the time they got here, but I couldn't just give up either. Living two hours out of town had it's benefits, but fast service wasn't one of them. Dammit. I let him get away. Fatima hadn't said a word since he fled from the scene. But I knew what she was thinking. She regretted pushing so hard. She regretted not accepting my rejection when I told her no. She hoped her life could go back to the way it was before she met me. If I could go back in time, I'd protect her from the poison that was me. No one deserved the life I've lived. Especially not a beautiful, and innocent woman like her. I was so lost in my thoughts. I forgot the police had arrived.

"Sir. I'm Officer Moore. We received a call saying there was an intruder in the home?" He spoke matter-of-factually with his hand propped comfortably on his right holster. His gray hair, thick mustache, and staunch posture suggested he was a veteran amongst rookies. I was glad to see they sent a big dog.

"He is already gone. It's been about two hours since he took off. I tried to follow him, but I was too slow." I swept my hands over my injures. It was obvious why I couldn't keep up.

"You say he left over two hours ago. What are

we looking for? Did he leave on foot, or by motor vehicle? Any details you can give us will help."

"I can't say. After our tussle downstairs. I limped my way to the second floor and found him. In the middle of ..." I couldn't find the words to say what I saw. It was like they were lodged down deep, and I could get a hold of them.

"He was raping me upstairs. Before Marcus came to my rescue. He charged him. And Darius went flying out the window. We both looked out the window, and he was already gone." Fatima answered for me. The room started spinning, and my vision began to fade. I grabbed my neck, and realized my make shift tourniquet was soaked in blood.

"Sir please have a seat.," an EMT said, arriving just in time. I listened from the couch, while Fatima told them what happened.

"Ma'am, you say you knew the assailant," a young officer inquired?

Fatima hesitated. Everything that happened was too much for her. I was used to death and violence. My whole childhood was filled with it, thanks to growing up with a monster. She had no idea how to deal with situations like last night. She must have been in shock, after hearing about what happened to Eddie, last night. When I told her the story, I never dreamed she would ever meet Darius. She couldn't process so much information about someone she never met. Now there asking her more questions about him. I'm sure the facts were more than a little gray.

"Yes officer. That's what she said. She's never met him in person. I told her about him, though." I interjected from the couch.

"Sir, please relax," the blonde working on me said, gently.

"Yes sir. He is correct. Marcus said, he was his brother." Fatima answered.

"Do you remember anything specific about him? Could you see any tattoos, or distinguishable markings on his body?"

"No. But he wore a night vision mask," she answered while looking down at her bloody knuckles.

"When we were fighting downstairs, it felt like he had on armor or something, too." I added.

The officers looked to each other sceptically. Our description of the night's events made him sound like a comic book super villain. But we were telling the truth with no extras.

Office Moore crossed his arms, and said, "Let me get this straight. Neither of you saw his face, but you claim the assailant was a man that was found dead last night?"

I limped across the room and stood inches away from his face. I wasn't going to let him make her or me feel inferior. "Look officer. It has been a long night, and now morning. We've told you everything we know, without any embellishments. If you have any further questions you can reach me at Kids First Pediatrics, I'm the attending physician there, or at home." I knew mentioning I was a doctor would shut the bullshit down fast. I didn't want to deal with anymore crap today.

"No problem, sir. We don't want to give you anymore trouble. We can't treat your brother as suspect for obvious reasons though. I'll have to visit the coroner to make sure the body identified in his home, is in fact his. If it's not, we can consider adding him as a suspect. Rest assured, we'll get to the bottom of this."

I didn't respond. I simply nodded.

Officer Moore tipped his hat, pivoted, and headed out the front door with three rookies following behind him.

"Ma'am. We need to take you in. So we can perform a rape kit." The EMT called out to Fatima.

The look in her eyes told me, she didn't want to go. How could I blame her? I'm sure, it would feel like being raped all over again. "That won't be necessary. I can get everything I need to do the kit from the hospital. I'll send in the results myself." I said directing everyone towards the door. I could see Fatima's shoulders drop in relief.

"Thank you babe," she said, joining me on the couch. It was going to be more than a long couple of days.

Chapter 3

Fatima

With my finger on the trigger, inside of my purse, I opened the door and strolled into my old apartment. Darius wasn't going to catch me off guard again. If he decided to show up, I had six hot ones waiting for his ass in the chamber. I just needed the opportunity to send them flying his way. I replayed all the possible outcomes, before deciding to come here alone. I could have asked Trina, Shana, or Denise to come along, but they would have asked too many questions. Mainly, who was Marcus, and what happened to Darius? I wasn't prepared to answer either question. Of course, Marcus would have been a great support, but I couldn't risk him finding a photo or evidence of me and his brother's relationship. I burned everything I could find, but you never know. I could have forgotten something. It simply wasn't worth the risk.

The last place I wanted to be on earth was here. But I had to make sure the movers got everything out, before I could collect my security deposit. I had only been gone for about a week, but it felt like forever since I'd been inside this house. I looked around, and thought about how happy I used to be living here. Back in the day, things felt so perfect. Before Darius lost his mind. Before Tasha betrayed me. And before I found out my entire life was lie. The memories were so bitter sweet, I didn't know what to do with them. I just wanted everything from my past to disappear.

The barrage of memories coming my way, made me so grateful to have Marcus in my life. He was kind enough to let me stay with him as long as I wanted. He even offered to have everything packed, moved, and shipped to his place. We only knew each other for about two weeks, but instantly we connected. His generosity amazed me. Before I could ask for what I needed, he already had it in hand. He wanted me to be near him at all times, which was great, because I didn't want to be alone. So it worked. My old self would have felt smothered or overwhelmed. Thank goodness, the naive gullible person I was died with the lies in this house. Even though, our relationship was brand new, my gut told me it was the real thing. I made the mistake of ignoring my intuition in the past, I wasn't going to make the same mistake again.

My footsteps bounced off the empty walls as I walked around my apartment. I saved the worse room for last. I peaked inside the bedroom setup for me and Darius's future baby, and negative emotions consumed me. My stomach twisted into a thousand knots. I felt my breakfast fighting to come up. The thought of having his baby literally made me sick. I told the mover's to sell or throw away all the baby stuff in the house, because I certainly wasn't going to need it. I was relieved to see they did. How could I have been so naive? He didn't even know him. Even though, we lived together for three years. We might as well have been strangers. I certainly learned my lesson. Time wasn't an indication of a healthy relationship. Darius taught me that.

As I turned to leave, I saw something out of the corner of my eye. I pivoted, and nearly fell over. I couldn't believe what I was seeing. Darius was standing on the other side of my patio doors with a wicked grin on his face. My brain didn't know what to do. It was like all my thoughts were caught in a traffic jam, and known of them could switch lanes, or find a way out. I had to be losing my mind. I ran my hand over my face, and shook my head. I hoped I was hallucinating, but I wasn't. He was still standing there laughing at me like this was a game. My palm began to sweat on the grip of the gun, and the steel trigger felt wet in my hand. Was it really him? Or was my eyes playing tricks on me? I couldn't be sure. I kept my eyes closed for a few seconds. Then I opened them again. His was attempting to pull the door open. I wasn't delusional. He was coming to finish the job. Tiny chill bumps ran over my body. He wasn't going to attack me again. I closed my eyes. Aimed. And pulled the trigger.

POP! POP! POP!

21

CRASH!

Glass went flying everywhere. I opened my eyes, and he was no longer standing there. Where the hell did he go? I dropped the gun in my purse, and ran across the living room. No one was standing on the patio balcony. There was only broken pieces of aluminum and glass on the ground. Across the way, I could see a lonely tree blowing in the wind. Oh my god. It wasn't over. He was stalking me.

BANG! BANG! BANG!

"Open up! It's the police!" A voice yelled from the other side of the door.

"Open up! Or were coming in."

My throat dried up, and I couldn't speak. What the fuck could I say? I knew he was here, but they wouldn't believe me. They didn't even think he was alive. A hawk of a man kicked down the door and bum-rushed inside. Then, he shoved the tip of his gun on my forehead. He peered down at me like he was ready to shot. I was so scared, I couldn't control my bladder.

"Put your hands up. And don't move."

My hands flew up immediately. I wasn't going to question a thing he said. Going to jail wasn't an option. If he asked me to stand on the ceiling, I would have given it a shot, because I wasn't cut out to do time. The officer standing behind him used his gun to motion towards the piss running down my leg. Then the hawk retreated.

"What the hell is going on here?" Officer Moore asked, standing in front of the door.

The trigger happy cop holstered his gun, and began to stammer.

"Spit it out son. What the hell were you doing?" Officer Moore yelled only inches from his face.

I didn't care, what was going on between them. I just wanted to run home and cry. My worst nightmare came true, plus more. Darius was stalking me. And there was nothing I could do about it. Now, I was standing in piss like a psych patient.

"Ms. Butler. I apologize for his reaction, instead of response. These idiots are going to search the premises while we talk. Please explain what happened?"

I crossed my legs at the ankle, and stuttered through my words. "I thought I saw Darius," was all could say.

He looked at me with sympathy in his eyes, then simply shook his head. "Ma'am, have you thought about seeing someone? It's okay to admit you need help. You've been through a lot. It's not easy getting over the type of stuff you've been through."

"I have," I lied. The look he gave me said he wasn't convinced. But thankfully, he didn't push the issue. I didn't want talk to him or anyone else. Darius was standing there smirking at me. I saw him just as clearly as I did Officer Moore, and the other two cops.

"I was planning on giving you and Mr. Du Bois a visit today. We ran the prints at the lab, and the results came back this morning. There is a 99.99 percent chance the man found in the fire was Darius. You don't have to worry about him raising from the ashes ma'am. There is no doubt, he is dead."

"Okay." I wasn't going to tell him he was wrong. The facts weren't up for debate. I'd know his body, scent, and voice anywhere. But I knew it didn't matter what I said. Since he already thought I was crazy. I had to admit, things weren't looking too good for me right now. I didn't give Darius enough credit. He was much smarter than I thought. Somehow, he managed to become the invisible man overnight. Now, there was hardly anything I could do to stay safe.

"Office Miles and Green, are going to follow you home. I'll call maintenance to explain what happened. Please get some rest, and try to recover. It's okay to take some time for yourself. Especially after such a traumatic event."

I nodded, grabbed my purse off the floor, and headed towards the door.

"One more thing ma'am. I'll need your gun."

I gave it to him. Then ran to my car. Embarrassed, didn't explain how I felt.

*****

I pulled into the driveway, and saw Marcus's car. Dammit. Why wasn't he at work? I slammed my hands on the steering wheel in frustration. How was I going to explain the patrol car following behind me, and the smell of piss permeating from my clothes. I got out the car, and prepared to run inside. I would just have to figure out a way to avoid him. Until I got out the shower. Both officers tipped their hats, and leaned against their patrol cars, as I walked inside. They were ordered to setup shop outside of our house, just in case Darius, excuse me, the unknown suspect, decided to comeback. I did feel a little safer knowing they were around.

I crossed my fingers and turned the door knob. Hopefully, he'd be upstairs. As soon as I stepped through the door, he was standing in front of me with a cheesy grin on his face. He was brandishing a piece of paper like it was the winning power ball numbers.

"Welcome home!" he chided.

"Hi." I said, rushing pass him, into the bathroom downstairs. I shut, and locked the door behind me.

"Hey," he followed, and banged on the door. "What's the matter? Have you been peeing like a Russian race horse?" He still had an annoying laugh in his voice. What hell was there to be happy about. I wasn't in the mood for jokes.

I pulled off my clothes, and I turned on the water. I wasn't in the mood to talk. Once I was out of the shower. I wrapped in a thick white towel, and realized I didn't have any clean clothes to put on. When I came out, he was sitting in his favorite chair. He definitely wasn't looking enthusiastic anymore.

"I'm sorry about what happened earlier. The officers explained why you were in such a shitty mood, when you came home." He clasped my hands, and lead me to the couch.

"You don't have anything to be sorry about. You didn't know what happened. And I was too embarrassed to tell you." I hated making him feel bad. Marcus was such a good man. If only he knew, I didn't deserve his kindness. I didn't tell him about me and Darius, the plan to con him, or anything else. He was still convinced the other night was his fault, because of the bad blood between them. But I knew the truth. Darius was coming to make good on his promise. In his world, I was his property, and Marcus stole me away. He swore he'd never let me go. And I believed him.

Marcus smiled weakly, but didn't respond. It was obvious, I sucked the happiness right out of him. He seemed excited to talk when I came home. Maybe telling me the good news would lift his mood. I can't image anything positive coming out of this situation, though.

"Fatima, you trust me don't you?" he said, breaking my thoughts.

"Of course."

"Good." His gripped my hands tightly and looked down at them. His serious attitude was really starting to freak me out. What the hell did he want to say.

"Marcus. Just tell me already. It's been a long day. You're going to give me a heart attack."

"I got the kit results today." Oh my god. He gave me the monster. I knew it. Darius was fucking around with that nasty bitch Tasha. There was no telling what that bitch had.

"I have HIV. I can't believe it." tears started rolling down my face.

"No … No. babe. Are you crazy. You're clean. We're going to have a baby." I swear the words left his lips in slow motion. I was happy to find out I didn't have any diseases, but relief and joy didn't overtake my body. Instead I felt fear and regret. I was with both of them so close together. It would be impossible to determine which one was the father.

"Aren't you excited."

I threw my hands around his neck, and hugged him tightly. I couldn't bare lying to him anymore. We both held each other, and cried for different reasons. What the hell was I going to do with a baby?

Chapter 4

Fatima

No one came out of the building the same. I watched from across the street as women dodged past protestors carrying signs, and bibles in their hands. Some entered as aggressively as the people demonstrating outside. Others held their head down in shame. I knew which category I'd fall under. Abortion was never an option to me, but I was definitely pro-choice. I certainly didn't agree with the government making medical decisions. I just never considered it an option for myself, especially considering my family background.

I should have been grateful to be pregnant. I setup a room for my imaginary baby, and even spent hundreds of dollars preparing for him or her. So why couldn't I imagine carrying to full term? I couldn't even picture myself being a mom, anymore. Plus, I wanted to be married before getting pregnant. Now, I was no different than those chicks on Maury. I didn't know if Marcus or Darius was the father of my child. I couldn't even say the reality out loud, I was so ashamed. What would I do, if Darius was the father?

Most of the time, I spent with him was amazing.

I couldn't lie. It was the truth. As much as it pained me to admit it. Looking back, I still didn't understand what happened to him. At some point, he turned into a different person. On second thought, he wasn't even human anymore to me. He was just a beast, or personal tormentor that wouldn't set me free. The possibility of this being his child was too much to bare. How could I carry such a thing inside of me? Rationally I knew it wasn't the baby's fault, but my heart wouldn't believe it. I still screamed his name, in my sleep. The things he did to me I could never forget. How could I move on, if I had to look at his child's face everyday? I didn't know if I could.

There was no way, I could have created a better hell for myself. How the hell did I fuck up my life so bad? Marcus was an innocent victim. He didn't even know half of what was going on. Every time he woke up in the middle of the night to buy me chocolate mint ice cream, because I was having a pregnancy craving, I wanted to scream, "The baby isn't yours. I'm a piece of shit. You should leave me." If I had a moral bone in my body, I would say just that, and paid the consequences. The problem was I needed him. I couldn't survive without him. The night terrors, and panic attacks were getting so bad. I rarely left the house. I was either scared Marcus would find out about our relationship, or Darius would pop up and kill me. Getting an abortion would probably be the best thing for everyone involved, including the baby. This child couldn't survive the mess I created. There was no other choice, I had to go through with it. Marcus shouldn't be tied down to me, because of what I did. He deserved someone honest and decent, not a liar like me.

I walked into the clinic, and saw women of every shade. Some even had swollen bellies. I was surprised to see them there, because I felt bad already being three months along. You couldn't tell I was pregnant, though, because of my height. I signed in, and sat down with the rest of the woman, who were scared to death.

"Fatima," the receptionist called from behind the counter. I said a silent prayer, and followed her to the examination room.

*****

"Welcome home!" everyone shouted when I walked through the door. Confetti and horns blew in my face. I was so caught off guard, I nearly jumped out of my skin. Marcus had completely out done himself. The living room was filled with yellow and gray balloons. It looked like a cute bubble bee convention. There was bubble cake, juice, cups, and plates. I couldn't have decorated better myself. I scanned the room, and saw my old friends standing in the back. How did Marcus find them? Trina, Shana, and Denise rushed over to give me hug. I could tell they were genuinely happy to see me.

"Do you like it?" he asked, pulling me into a warm embrace.

"I do. Thank you. You didn't have to do this."

"Of course, I did. I want you to be happy."

Looking around the room, I realized half the people I didn't even know. Still, the thought was sweet. I recognized Amy from his office, and of course the girls, but everyone else were complete strangers.

"Tell me the truth. Is this okay?" he asked, motioning around the room. "It seems like you've been having a hard time. I hope you're not mad, I invited everyone over. I thought you should have some fun without worrying. So, I brought the party to you. Besides, I wanted to tell everyone about the baby. I couldn't keep the secret anymore."

"Of course, I'm not mad. I do have to use the bathroom though." I pecked him on the cheek, handed him my bag, and escaped to the upstairs bathroom. I could feel a panic attack coming on.

God, I hated getting setup. If I wanted Denise, Trina, and Shana to know my business I would have told them. The last thing I wanted to come home to was a roomful of people. I could careless if I knew them or not, I just wanted to be left alone. Marcus was always surprising me with something sweet. He meant well, but this time he was completely off the mark. I didn't want to celebrate anything. Especially not pregnancy. I wanted to come home, and zone out on trash television. Now I had to deal with this shit. Yeah, he was trying to do something sweet for me, but it only made me feel worse. I needed some space to figure my shit out.

Boom! Boom! Boom!

"What?" I yelled. Someone was beating on the door like they lost their damn mind.

"Open up Fatima!"

I swung the door open, and saw Marcus was pissed. His eyes were razor sharp, and he looked like he was on a war path.

"What the hell is this?" I was literally speechless. He was thrusting my appointment card from the clinic in my face. It must have fallen out of my bag, when I handed it to him. I was in such a hurry to get upstairs, I must have dropped it. I could hear people saying their goodbyes, and leaving downstairs. Apparently, he was ready to fight.

"Answer me. What is this, Fatima?"

"Baby, let me explain." My mind was racing, I

had no idea what to say. I just knew I needed to say something. So he would calm down.

"Go ahead. I'm listening."

I was still drawing a blank. Anything I said, wouldn't sound good. He was pissed, and had every right to be. "It's not what it looks like babe." I couldn't think of anything better. He threw his hand up, and cut me off.

"You want to kill our child Fatima. Why? What the hell did I ever do to you?" he stood in the doorway with tears in his eyes. I really fucked up this time. The last thing I wanted to do was hurt him. I scheduled the appointment, because I didn't want to get in his way. How could explain my situation. I could tell him Darius forced me to date him, that the only reason we met was so I could con him out of his inheritance, or that I couldn't refuse because he threatened to rape me, if I didn't fall in line. None of those answers would make him feel better. So why tell him? Instead, I lied. It was kinder.

"Marcus, I'm sorry. I don't know what else to say. I was stupid. I made a mistake."

He got on his knees, and placed his ear against my belly. "Please tell me you didn't do it, Fatima. I need both of you to keep me going. I can't handle anymore bullshit." I'd never seen Marcus cry. Even after the attack, he didn't shed a tear. I really felt like a piece of shit for what I did.

"I didn't do it. Marcus. The baby is okay."

"Thank god." he said, wrapping his arms around my waist. He was breathing so hard, I could feel his heart beating against my thigh.

"I'm sorry, baby. I know you've been through a lot too. I didn't want to add to your stress. I thought, your life would be easier, without us."

He stood up, and grabbed my face with both of his hands. "Listen to me Fatima. I don't want you to go anywhere. You're my family. It's just me, you, and this baby." he said, putting his hand on my stomach. "I need you to believe that. Yeah. We had a rocky start. But our love is real. If we can survive that night, our relationship is ironclad, and unbreakable." He squeezed me like he was I afraid I would disappear.

I wanted to deserve everything he said, but the truth was I didn't. Even my body rejected his words. My chest was so tight, and full of tears, I just refused to let any of them fall. He treated me like fine china, not realizing I was the one responsible for his pain. His generosity and love, only made me feel worse. Darius couldn't hurt Marcus directly. He would have seen him coming. He needed me to play my part in order to solve his legal problems. If I stole the money, and returned to Darius like he wanted. Marcus wouldn't have gotten hurt. We would be living in separate houses. And this baby wouldn't exist. Instead, I've entangled him in Darius's web. There was no way he would leave us alone, now that I'm pregnant. Finding out would only fuel his fire. I couldn't bare lying to him anymore. I needed to tell him the truth. He didn't love me. He only thought he did. He didn't know why we met, or what my intentions were that night.

"Marcus, I have something to tell you. I hope you can understand why I went to the clinic."

"You don't have to explain anything to me Fatima. I just want you promise you'll take care of our child."

My voice started to shake, but I wasn't going to stop now. He needed to hear what I had to say. "That's the thing. I went to the clinic, because I didn't know if you or Darius was the father of my baby."

"Fatima. Stop worrying. There's no way Darius is the father. The blood work showed your were already a few weeks pregnant, the night of the attack. We're good. Just be happy, okay." He planted a soft kiss on my lips, and hugged me tight. I couldn't believe his response. My willpower was gone. I couldn't muster up the strength to say it again. So, I left it at that.

Chapter 5

Marcus

AAH!

Jarred out of my sleep, I shot up in bed. Damn. I hadn't gotten a good night's sleep in months, which was really starting to wear on me. I had to hire a partner to take over some of my patients at work. Even though, I hated to do it. I had no other choice. I kept having to run home because she needed me. The panic attacks were nonstop. They consumed her day and night. Nothing seemed to help. As much as I want to understand where she was coming from, it was difficult. The attack happened over six months ago. I knew how bad it was. I was there, but I thought we could commemorate, but she wouldn't even talk to me about it. I even offered to pay for therapy, medication, or whatever she needed, but she refused to go. I didn't know what the hell to do. I even bought a shot gun, rifle, and .45 to make her feel safer. But none of it seemed to restore her faith in me.

"No! No!" Her bone chilling scream filled the room. I was shaking her arm, but she wasn't waking up.

"Fatima! Fatima! I'm here. Do you here, babe?

Wake up." I rubbed her forehead, when she was coming to. She was so into the dream, her body was drenched in sweat. I rubbed her swollen belly, and felt our little girl squirm. I hoped to god, she wasn't as stressed out as her mom.

"Marcus." Fatima sighed deeply. I could feel the stress lifting off her shoulders, and onto mine. Within seconds, she feel back to sleep. It was like a revolving door. The same thing happened last night, and the night before that, and so on. This shit had to stop.

I moseyed down the staircase, then poured myself a shot of whiskey. What else could I do? I wasn't much of a drinker, or at least I didn't used to be. But lately, I'd been reaching for the bottle more, and more. I guess the stress was getting to me. Even though, Darius had apparently disappeared, his presence was still felt. Fatima was consumed with him. I couldn't even take my own woman out. Every time I suggested going out for dinner, a movie, or even a stroll down the street, she would flip out and start talking about bumping into him. I got a license to carry. I knew the area. I was capable of protecting her, and our baby. Why couldn't she have faith in me? I took another swig of whiskey, and thought about the state of my life. I would never lose my woman and child again. I wish she could understand that.

Life gave me another chance to prove I could

keep my family safe. And I was determined to succeed this time. I knew I made mistakes in the past, but I wouldn't repeat them. The night Darius took Eddie out, I was awake. I could have gotten out of bed, and told him to stop – but I was too much of a coward, even back then. It shouldn't have mattered he was crazy. I should have met him every step of the way. Instead, we hardly talked, even though we shared room. I got so freaked out, because of the crazy shit he did like stuffing our cat inside the dryer. Then, turning it on. I still remember the smell of our cat's rotting flesh. It never got out of the walls, no matter how much my mom tried to clean it. Regardless, I could have at least tried to stop him. Even if he beat my ass like he usually did. Worst case scenario, my parents would have woken up, and Eddie would still be alive. Darius was only a year older than me, but he was six years older than Eddie. I should have been his protector. He didn't stand a chance scraping with him. He was just a little kid. I slammed my fist on the table, and I doubled up. It was the only thing that could take the edge off the pain.

"Baby, is everything okay?" she asked, standing across the room. She looked even more beautiful carrying my child than she did before. My heart swelled up just thinking about her.

"I'm fine," I said, trying to steady my words. I definitely didn't want to give her anything else to worry about.

"What's wrong baby?" she wrapped her arm around my neck, and rubbed my chest. I could never lie to her. She always knew when something was wrong.

"Don't worry about me. Worry about you." I planted a soft kiss on her lips. "And our little princess." I said, kissing her belly button.

"Marcus, come to bed." She tried to pull me off the bar stool, but I wasn't going anywhere. I couldn't waking up to her screams. It was driving me crazy.

"I'll be right behind you babe. Go ahead without me."

"You said that last night. And I found you asleep on the couch in the morning."

"Fatima please. Just go back to bed." She crossed her arms. I knew then, getting her to go back to sleep wasn't going to be easy.

"I don't know what's gotten into you lately. You've hardly been eating. You don't want to come to bed anymore. Tell me what's wrong."

She asked for the truth, but I knew she couldn't handle it. I couldn't remember the last time we made love. Every time, I touched her, she pulled away. It was like I repulsed her. When I brought it up to her in the past, she blamed it on the pregnancy, but I saw the look on her face. Her eyes were wide and full of terror. It was like she was looking into the eyes of a monster. I couldn't help wondering if she saw him when she looked in my eyes. We do look similar, as much as I hated to admit. It felt like she wasn't even mine. Like I was sleeping with another man's woman, with his woman, not mine. Even though, I was the one running her bath water, rubbing her swollen feet, and feeding her when she was hungry. He still had her heart clutched in his fist, and I couldn't get to it. No matter how hard I tried.

"Babe. I don't want to do this tonight. Just go back to bed."

"Do what Marcus? What is this? I just want to know what's wrong?"

"What isn't wrong Fatima? You can't sleep without waking up screaming. You haven't left the house since what happened. We don't have sex. I don't even remember what it feels like. But you want to know what's wrong." I slammed down my shot glass, and paced the floor. I didn't want to do this with her.

"So all this is because of me? Why didn't you just say so, huh? I don't have to stay here, if you don't want me to. I can leave." Her eyes welled up with tears, and her fingers started trembling. We both knew, she had no place to go.

41

"I'm not saying everything is your fault … a man has needs. It's as simple as that." Before she came into my life, I was celibate. But that was different. I wasn't thinking about love, sex, or relationship. I was completely engulfed in my work. Laying with her at night was torture. I wanted to kiss her sweet lips, full breasts, and that honey pot between her legs, but every time I tried, it turned into a fight.

"So your punishing me, because I won't have sex with you?" I couldn't believe it. Was she smoking crack. Everything I did was for her. I came downstairs, because I didn't want to disturb her, and that made me selfish.

"Are you out of your mind? What do you want me to do Fatima?"

"Come to bed."

"I can't take it anymore. You're driving me crazy." Instantly, her face was filled with sadness. I didn't want to fight. I just needed a break. Fatima stood there with tears in her eyes. I had to make things better for the both of us.

"Come here." I said, pulling her into my chest. I brushed her hair as she cried in my arms. We were both such a fucking mess. The last year was bitch. I wanted to be strong for the both of us, but it was hard. It seemed like everyday was battle. It didn't help that she reminded me so much of my mom which really scared the hell out of me. I didn't want her to meet the same fate.

After Darius killed my Eddie. Our family was destroyed. He was shipped off to juvenile hall, but he wasn't the only one punished. It was like we all died right along with Eddie. My dad was never home. He lived at the church, but he wasn't only there to deliver the good news. No. Half the congregation had a piece of Mr. Du Bois and everybody knew it. We constantly had woman volunteering to clean our house, wash our clothes, and cook dinner. They said it was to help the first lady, but I knew what was up. I couldn't count the times I found my dad in compromising positions. My poor mom was too gone to even notice. As a kid, I hated my dad. I couldn't understand how cheated. As a man, I could honestly say, I didn't blame him. He still had needs. Besides, being around my mom was unbearable. She just wasn't the same after his death. In fact, she wasn't even a shell of her former self. All she did was reminisce or hallucinate about the good old days. My dad tried his best to stand by her, but nothing he tried helped. She was prescribed all kinds of medications. All of them, she abused. Half the time, I expected to find her dead when I came home from school. But somehow, she survived. I didn't understand how she outlived my old man. I refused to let history repeat itself. Fatima would have to get better. She had no other choice. Our baby deserved the best, and neither of us were up to par at the moment.

Fatima whipped her face, and looked into my eyes. "I promise to do better, okay," she actually looked sincere. I'm sure she'd try, but I certainly wasn't going to get my hopes up. After all, we were technically still in the honeymoon faze, and we had already been through so much. If this was the good times, I definitely didn't want to see the bad. I'd support her as much as I could. Hopefully, she'd make good on her word.

Chapter 6

Darius

Tasha spread out the foil, dropped the crystal, lit it, and inhaled like a champion. I smacked her bare ass lying across the bed, and she turned around holding a ball of smoke in her mouth. She pressed her lips against mine, and exhaled. We'd been charging, and fucking all night. I felt like a kid again. I surveyed her body, and had to admit, she looked amazing after having three kids. Her body was stacked and fat ass fuck. A nigga couldn't hold a nut, messing around with her. She was a certified freak. The girl practically lived on her knees. Don't get it twisted, I for damn sure wasn't complaining. But, her ass was what drove me wild. I shook my head just thinking about that donkey sitting on her back. I'd been chilling with her for the last few weeks to recuperate from the madness. I needed to come up with another game plan. A little ass, and a hint of smoke was just what I needed to get my mind right. I grabbed another handful, before sitting up to watching the nightly news.

Officers found Emily Bronson face down and nude inside her Rose Creek Addition home. Neighbors, family, and friends haven't been able to provide deputies with any plausible suspects.

Crimes like this never happen in this neighborhood. No one knows what to think. A candlelight vigil will be held later tonight in her memory. People in the community describe her as a great mother, wife, friend, and community pillar. She was an active PTA member, and volunteer at New Beginning Ministries. No one can understand how an outstanding citizen like her was attacked so brutally. Let alone in her own home. Police weren't able to find any signs of forced entry. It appears, she knew her attacker well enough to invite him or her inside. Sadly, her husband and three children found her manned body, after returning home. Here is a few words from her grieving spouse.

Emily didn't deserve this. I can't believe someone would do such a thing to her. She was innocent. And a good person. Why did she have to die so young. (Inaudible) If you have any information that can help police find her killer, please, pickup the phone now. Don't wait. We need your assist immediately, while the trail is still hot. We can't afford to let this monster run free on the streets.

I clicked off the television and laughed. Television was definitely the right word. They were certainly telling visions, because that broadcast was full of lies. I'm sure Emily was a lot of things, but innocent, for damn sure wasn't one of them. I usually have to blaze a trail for Mr. King Snake, but

46

her road was already paved, and ready to go. The bitch did give phenomenal head though.

"Momma when is Tavia and Nikki coming back?" little man asked with his cup in hand. I could always depend on four things from Tasha: good food, nice smoke, mediocre pussy, and lip. Being an acceptable mother to my son, wasn't on the list. I couldn't trust her to raise him right. She had her nappy-headed kids beating him up everyday. They had to go. Those little bitches weren't going to be shit anyway. They were just taking up space. Besides, I wasn't trying to be around another niggas kids, anyway. What type of girls hit on their little brother? They were acting like dikes, and hadn't even left the nest yet. I gave Tasha two options: she could drop them off somewhere, or allow me to handle the situation. As expected, she had them, and their shit packed in flash.

"Momma," he continued to whine. She didn't respond. Her sandy brown her was laid out and covering her face. She didn't have any clothes on. Neither of us did. She was butt naked, and faced down on the bed. Everywhere you looked, shit was thrown. Tasha's room was always a pit. I pushed on the back of her head, but she didn't move. Was this stupid bitch dead?

"Tasha! Tasha!" I yelled, but she didn't respond. DeMarcus started screaming and crying. The plate

on the night stand didn't have any dope on it. A
pool of frothy drool was in her mouth.

"Get out!" I yelled, while flipping her over. He
ran behind me, and starting screaming even louder.
I flung his ass against the wall. He didn't need to
see what was going on. Besides, I didn't have time
to explain shit him, at the moment. Tasha was
burning up. I couldn't let her die. I still need her
help to fulfill my plan.

I ran to the bathroom, and filled up the tub with
cold water. I needed to shock her system. We had a
couple of bags of ice in the freezer, I decided to
throw them inside too. A ran back to the room,
threw her over my shoulder, and dumped her in the
tub.

She started flopping like a fish immediately. I
sighed in relief. I thought she was dying. I couldn't
have her stupid ass, ruining my plans. She was
holding onto the side of the tub, trying to catch her
breath. I put her in a headlock, until her face turned
purple.

"If you ever do that shit again, I'll kill you,
okay?" A tear rolled down her eye, and she nodded
with the quickness. I let her ass go, and she quickly
grabbed at her neck. Her bright complexion
returned to her face. And little man ran into the
room, and threw his arms around her. I hated for
him to see his mom like that. But I couldn't let her

ruin my plans.

Everything in my life was perfect, before I started messing with her ass. Business was great. Me and Fatima were looking forward to our life together. Everything was really looking up. Every now and again, I had to deal with the voices in my head, but that wasn't anything new. They'd been with me since I was a little kid. I learned how to keep them in check. They rarely caused problems or affected my daily life.

If it wasn't for Fatima's bright idea, life would still be good right now. She just couldn't wait to introduce me to Tasha. I remember the day we met. As soon as I saw her, I knew they weren't related. Fatima was tall, slender, and top heavy. She looked like a model. Tasha on the other hand, looked like a your typical video ho. They both looked good, but served different purposes. Fatima was the type you brought to Christmas parties, and conferences. Tasha was definitely a side chick, or back burner at best. I knew Tasha was trouble as soon as I saw her. It wasn't the body that gave it away. It was her demeanor. She had slut written all over her. Fatima was just too naive to see it. She didn't have any respect for her. Her breast were always spilling out of her tops. I don't think I every saw her wearing anything, but skinny jeans that displayed every dangerous curve she possessed. Bringing her around was like putting a smoked Christmas ham in front of starved dog. Anybody would have taken a bite.

I remember the first day Fatima introduced us. Her face lit up when she talked about her girl. She even called Tasha her sister. Apparently, they roomed together as teenagers, since they were both runaways. Fatima was tired of living in shelters and boarding houses. As soon as she hit puberty, no one wanted to take her on as a foster child. She was tall, and developed early. Women didn't want her in their home. It would have been too much temptation for their sons and husbands. I couldn't blame them. My girl was sexy as fuck. That was why she decided to pack her shit, and hit the streets. Somewhere along the way she met Tasha.

From what she told me, Tasha's background was no better. Her mom had men running in and out the house. Many of them paid Tasha a visit when the lights went out. She tried to tell her mom, but she didn't care. She just kept on doing her thang. You'd think Tasha would decide to be better than her mom. Nope. Instead, she became just like her. Word got around, she'd do anything for a price. Shortly after, she became pregnant. After the second time, her mom put her out on the streets. Soon after, she met Fatima. They were inseparable until I came along.

As bad as the story sounds, the fault didn't lie with me. Tasha was the master pulling the strings. I was a victim like Fatima. Anytime she left us alone, Tasha was on my nuts. At first it was subtle. She'd accidentally spill her drink in my lap. Then, she'd seductively clean me off. When Fatima got back, she would jumped up, of course. Somehow, she never got caught. Every time she approached me, I turned her down, but she only got more aggressive. She started calling me randomly for help. For example, her car broke down. So, she hit me up. She claimed I was the only one who could help her, because she didn't have a man in her life. Yeah right. I knew game when I saw it, but I went anyway. Her tire had a clean slash it. It couldn't have happened naturally. But I didn't crack her face. Actually, I thought it was funny. So I kicked her some cash, and put on her spare tire. Fatima never heard a word about it. I felt a little bad for not telling her, but it wouldn't have done anything but raise suspension. Alright. I admit, we fucked occasionally. But it was nothing serious. So I kept our little meetings to myself. I knew, I was wrong, but she needed my help. I couldn't leave a single mother stranded on the side of the road. At first, I was able to keep her in line without a problem. But then, my operation blew up.

When Eddie got arrested. I couldn't take the stress. I tried turning to Fatima for support, but she didn't get it. She kept going on about having a baby, and getting married. I couldn't think about family planning when I had my freedom on the line. There

51

were many things I loved about her. She was different than most woman I met. She didn't let bad experiences sour her sweetness. Even though, she didn't have family, she was the most nurturing person I ever met, next to my mom. I knew she'd be a perfect mother and wife someday. It just wasn't the right time. If only she understood that. Unfortunately, her head was too much in the clouds. She couldn't be there for me at the time. I had to look elsewhere for support.

My boy Tool was good at following directions. But his slow ass couldn't think his way out of a paper bag. So he wasn't any help. Then there was Tasha. She understood how gritty life could be. Sometimes life forced your hand to do things others wouldn't understand. When I was on the edge, she came to me barring everything I needed to decompress. The first time we got together, she rolled up a fatty laced with angle dust, and we conceived little man. I was enraged. I swore I'd never touch that shit again. But life got too hectic, and I reached for it again. For awhile, crystal was my girl. She calmed me down, and I was able to think clearer than before. But then, everything got worse. The voices in my head weren't listening. In fact, they got louder, and louder, until I couldn't control them anymore. If I would have stayed away from this bitch, things wouldn't have snowballed. I would be on top of the world, like I was before I met her ass. As far as I'm concerned, she orchestrated this whole situation. Now, it was her responsibility to fix it.

Chapter 7

Darius

"The receptionist said, she's six months along. They threw a baby shower and everything." Tasha said, sucking her teeth and crossing her arms.

I was overjoyed. Fatima was going to have my baby. I reached across the stick shift, and hugged her tightly. We were finally back on track. "Did you get a chance to see her? Is she big? I bet she doesn't even look pregnant? My girl always looks sexy as fuck?"

"She looked alright." She rolled her eyes, then stared out the window.

I backed handed her ass. "Bitch, I don't you need you putting dubs on shit. Just answer my fucking questions." I wanted to track Fatima myself, but after the incident at her apartment. I decided to back off. I didn't want her getting arrested, or shooting my ass. I had to be practical.

"I'm sorry." She yelled, grabbing her face.

Every once and awhile, Tasha got lippy. I had to make sure to keep her in line. Looking at her now, you couldn't tell she used to be fine. Her body was no longer thick. The dope was taking a toll on her beauty. I was seriously thinking about restricting her use. She needed to thicken up.

"Don't hit my mommy!" DeMarcus yelled, from the back seat.

"Punk, shut up." I said, laughing. I pushed him back in his seat, and started smoking a laced blunt. He little ass thought he was hard.

Tasha had been doing recon missions for awhile. DeMarcus had to go to his well child appointment. It was the perfect opportunity to get information on Fatima. I knew Fatima didn't tell Marcus about our plan to con him out of his money. If she did, I'm sure they wouldn't be together. Fatima had to be scared, because Tasha never saw her visiting Marcus at work. Apparently, she knew me better than I thought. I'd never give up on us. We were family. The fact that Marcus thought he could steal my girl, only made the game sweeter.

I needed to find away to move closer to her, without alerting the police. I wasn't about to let him raise my child. I wondered, if we were having a boy or girl. She always said, she wanted a little Darius. The memory brought a smile to my face. The mission was taking longer than I expected, but news of her pregnancy got my creative juices flowing again. I decide to make myself known.

"Did you find out anything else?" I asked, taking a long drag. Tasha wasn't paying attention. She was too busy picking at the soars on her arms. Her beauty was gone. Now the drugs were working on her mind. She wouldn't be any use for much longer. "Tasha. Did you find out anything else?" I repeated, agitated?

"I told you everything already. The receptionist didn't know anything else. I couldn't' even schedule a follow up appointment with Marcus. DeMarcus will have to see a new doctor the next time, he comes in. So I didn't schedule another appointment.

"Good girl," I said, passing the blunt. I found out everything I needed to make my next move. With Fatima being so far along, he'd be staying at home. So I couldn't strike there. It wasn't worth trouble striking at home. I'd have to get her another way. I'd been waiting to catch her outside, but she wasn't leaving the nest. I just had to stay patient. Eventually, she'd slip up. When she did, I'd be waiting in the cut.

*****

Marcus left for work about thirty minutes ago. I was posted on the main road from their house. Today was going to be the day I saw my girl again. I had Tasha befriend some of Fatima's old girlfriends from college on Facebook. She thought I didn't know about the nights she went partying with the girls, but I knew. I just wasn't showing her my full hand. I figured it was a calculated risk worth taking. She could have caught wind and closed down all her social media accounts, and I would have been without some valuable information. Thankfully I got lucky, and was provided with a healthy stream information. Not because of what she posted though. She hadn't been online for months. Her girlfriend Shana, on the other hand, basically posted whenever she took a shit. I knew their full schedule for the day, just from reading her public wall. They had food and shopping on the agenda today. So I planned on tagging along. It had been too long, since I paid my baby a visit.

Fatima pulled onto the main road, and I followed four car lengths behind her. I didn't want to rush back into her life just yet. Instead, I decided to gently make my presence known. She needed to remember some of the good times we had together, not just the bad. I could have easily kidnapped or forced her to be with me, but I didn't want to do that.

I wanted to show her how tough life would be with Marcus, or anyone else. She needed to learn from her mistakes, by dealing with the consequences of her actions. She needed to understand, why deciding to leave was a bad choice. And I planned on showing her why. I asked myself regularly, what the fuck was wrong with her? Why couldn't she understand how easy life would be, if we were together? She wouldn't have to live with her head on a swivel. She could relax and enjoy her life, knowing she was safe with me. I really loved her stupid ass, but she could be too stubborn at times. Unfortunately, she would have to learn her lessons the hard way. Lucky for her, I took an individualized approach. For months, I spent my time developing the perfect curriculum. I knew exactly what she needed to see the light. Strong motivation, direction, and a desirable reward would have her ass begging to come back home.

Fatima pulled into a plaza parking lot. There was a Korean nail shop, a liquor store, and other miscellaneous shops inside. She was there meeting her girlfriends at a home style diner. I'd eaten there a few times, an old white couple owned the place. They had the best yeast rolls, cornbread, and chicken around. My stomach started growling just thinking about the menu. She walked through door, and I thumbed through the Sunday paper while I waited. The diner was too small for me surveillance from inside. She would have immediately seen me coming if I went inside. The cover story read:

The Good Wife Killer

Authorities have connected three homicides with the murder that took place six months ago in Rose Creek Addition. Three other victims were found

with the same signature. All three victims were
happily married with children, and members of
affluent neighborhoods. The first victim Emily
Bronson was just thirty six years old, and found
dead in her kitchen. The second victim Crystal
Montgomery was a twenty eight year old, mother of
two. She was found dead in her master bedroom.
The last victim Barbara West was thirty two years
old. She had three kids, and was found dead in the
guest bedroom. We can't release details about the
killer's signature. Police have received several
false leads due to incorrect information, and copy
cat attempts ...

The article continued, but I read enough. They
weren't even close to being on the right track. I
needed to send a thank you card to whoever
decided to follow my lead, cause I didn't know any
of the other bitches. Killing Emily was a simple
solution to a complex problem. I wasn't anybody's
serial killer, though. In fact, I was insulted at the
implication. If I wanted to start slaying people, I
wouldn't just go after boring bitches in the burbs.
Where's the fun in that? Why make it obvious by
going after the same type of bitches? The Good
Wife Killer. That shit sounded corny ass fuck. They
could have come up with something better than
that. Regardless. It felt good knowing, I was still
the invisible man.

I was surprised the media was making such a big

deal out of Emily's death. I couldn't turn on the television, computer, or radio without somebody talking about finding her killer. They acted like the bitch was finding the cure to cancer. I rubbed my hands over the front of the paper. There was a large photo of Emily and her family on the front. I folded the rest of the people out of the frame, and reminisced about the time we spent together. The way her body jerked before taking her last breath was better than any drug, or bitch on the street. A warm sensation covered my body, as I allowed myself to relive the experience. The idea of another kill did sound good to me. In fact, just thinking about it made my dick hard. I had a thirst for more of the same, but that shit would have to wait for now, because I couldn't lose sight of my goal.

While Fatima was busy grubbing, and chopping it up with her friends, I decided to leave her a little present, for when she came back. I hopped out the car, and crept up to her vehicle. I picked up a greeting card, and wrote a special note inside. I wanted to let her know, I was excited about our new bundle of joy.

HONK! HONK! HONK!

The car went fucking bonkers. I fell on my ass, dropped the card, and jerked my head from side to side. I barely touched the fucking thing, and it started flipping out. All I did was try to slide the card in the lip of the window. I put it back in my pocket, and jetted across the parking lot, before anyone could come rushing out. I peered through the blacked out windshield from the drivers seat. I watched Fatima, she was only a few steps behind me, and her friends quickly followed behind her. She cupped her mouth, and threw her hands on top of her head. I didn't want to upset her. It wasn't good for the baby. I just wanted to let her know, I was excited to meet him or her. Besides her being upset, she looked more beautiful than I remembered. She had one of those sweater style maternity dresses on, and she wore her hair pulled up in a high bun. I watched as she surveyed the parking lot. I'm sure she was looking for me.

What the hell was going on? My eyes were bulging out of my head in shock. If my eyes weren't deceiving me, it appeared light was reflecting off her finger. I saw it again! I couldn't believe it. This muthafucker bought her a ring. I slammed my hands against the stirring wheel, and started punching the dashboard. Not only did he steal her from me, but he's trying to claim my child, and marry her ass, too. Oh hell nawl, this shit wasn't happening. He had me all the way fucked up. Shit just got real. I definitely needed to switch up my game plan. Since fourth quarters was over. And we were now in overtime. This game was too tight to call. I fucked around for way too long. It was time to wrap this shit up, asap.

Chapter 8

Fatima

"What the hell do you want?" I was pissed. I couldn't believe she had the nerve to show her face. Tasha was standing on my front porch, looking as pitiful as ever. She even had DeMarcus with her. I guess she figured, pulling on my heart strings would further her cause. I have to admit, it did a little bit, because if she was by herself, I would have slammed the door in her face already.

"I know, I'm the last person you want to see right now, but I have something important to tell you." Whatever she had to say, couldn't be important, because I could careless about what was going on in her life. I didn't know if the pregnancy hormones were getting to me, but I wasn't as mad as I put on. I never saw her look so bad in my life. I had my own problems to deal with. I didn't need her adding to my list of shit to do. Actually, that wasn't entirely true. She used to be so vivacious and lively. She never left the house without doing her hair and makeup. She actually ragged on me for not wearing the latest fashions like she did. Honestly, I looked better than her, even though I was six months pregnant. Something really had to be wrong for her to show up on my door step. Especially considering she looked so bad.

I stepped to the side, motioning for her to come in. I knew, I probably shouldn't have, but I still cared about her. Even though, she betrayed me. We used to be so close. I thought we'd grow old together, and reminisce about the good old days while talking in our rocking chairs. Her betrayal totally blind sided me. I really thought we were more than friends. It was crazy how our entire relationship collapsed over a piece of shit like Darius. I would've been a blessing if she met him first. Tasha sat down on the sofa with DeMarcus by her side. He used to be my little baby, I couldn't walk into the room without him jumping on my lap. It had been almost a year since we'd seen each other, he probably didn't even remember me. I rubbed my belly, and smiled at his little feet hanging off the couch.

"Do you want a snack or something to eat?" DeMarcus didn't look well at all. Whatever happened to her affected how she took care of him. Usually, he was full of smiles and giggles, but he seemed just a broken down as she did.

"No thank you, we ate before we came." Tasha lied.

"Uh huh, mommy. I'm hungry," he said, starting to cry.

"I'll get you something to eat baby." Any anger I

had, disappeared. She was sitting on my couch covered in soars and bruises. Her poor baby didn't look any better than the kids on the feed the children infomercials.

"Fatima, you don't have to do that." She said, as I headed into kitchen.

"Don't worry about it." I gave her a weak smile, and returned with ham sandwiches, chips, cookies, and a pitcher of lemonade for both of them. Tasha was so hungry she bit her tongue. And DeMarcus couldn't stop smiling he was so happy. I felt good knowing he had a full belly. I knew exactly what it felt like to be him. I missed plenty of meals growing up in foster care.

"Thank you so much," Tasha eyes began to water, but no tears fell down. I knew she was really broken, because she never allowed herself to look weak in front of anyone.

"Please. It's nothing. What's going on?"

"I want you to forgive me, Fatima. I shouldn't have done you like that. No man is worth our friendship."

"Tasha, all that's water under the bridge. I have so much going on right now, I'm not even thinking about the past." I lied straight through my teeth. The past was all I thought about. But she didn't need to know that. Even though, I felt bad for her. I still didn't trust her. She showed me who she was. I'd be stupid to forget it."

"Can we start over. I really need a friend right now. You know I don't have anybody else. It's always been me and you. Team Unwanted. Remember?" When were teenagers, we joked about the outcast. The ones nobody wanted. Now it sounded silly hearing her say that. We both were mothers, now. We could never been unwanted. In fact, we'd be needed for along as children lived, at the least. Suddenly, I realized she didn't have the girls with her. I wondered where they were.

"Tasha. Where's Octavia and Nikki? Did you make up with your mom?" She put her head down, and began to cry.

"Fatima. I fucked up. I really fucked up, girl." I got up, and started rubbing her back. In all the years I'd known her, she never cried. At least, not in front of me.

"What happened?"

"Where do I start? Things have been so bad, since we stopped talking. My world just started spinning out of control. For awhile, it was just me and the kids, but then he came back." A chill rushed down my spin, and I moved across the room into Marcus's chair.

"He? Who's he?" I had a good idea who she

meant, but I didn't want to say it.

"Darius," she said, putting her head down. "Darius, came back into my life about six months ago.

I really didn't want to hear anything else. I felt bad life her life wasn't going as planned, but I wasn't going to invite more trouble into mine, trying to help her. "I can't go there, Tasha. I think you should leave."

"Wait. I need a friend. Who else can I talk to? Everyone else doesn't even think he's alive." I knew how she felt. It was hard being tormented by a man in the shadows. She betrayed our friendship, which was unforgivable, but she was literally the only person who could understand my position.

"Go ahead," I said, sitting back down. "You've got fifteen minutes. Marcus will be home soon."

"I got a call from him, saying he needed a ride. I'd been crying for weeks, because they said he was dead on the news. As soon as I heard his voice, all common sense went out the window. I was too relieved to hear he was alive, and okay. Like an idiot, I rushed over to get him. But when I saw him, I was at a lost for words. He looked like the same old Darius, but he was missing a hand, and he was wearing strange clothes. I asked him about it, and he gave me a look that said shut the fuck up. So I did. After, I picked him up, my life was never the same."

I listened as Tasha described what happened. It made perfect sense. Office Moore said they had proof Darius was the man in the fire. Obviously they didn't, because he was still walking around. Maybe they identified his hand. I wanted to know everything about my opponent. In case he decided to show up. I wasn't dumb enough to think I knew who I was dealing with, Darius obviously wasn't the man I thought he was. I couldn't help thinking god was giving me a heads up while she was telling me the story.

"Before I knew it, he was threatening my kids. I didn't want to leave them," she started crying again. "What was I supposed to do? They weren't safe with me. It was like I invited the devil into my home. He took over everything. My house, my car, even my bank account was his. The only time I got away from him was at work. After awhile, I tried to resist. I told him, he needed to get his shit and leave. But he just laughed, and flexed his muscles. Everything is a fucking game to him."

I thought I was going to learn about his intentions, and how they could affect me, Marcus, and the baby. Apparently, she just wanted to get some stuff off her chest, which I didn't have time for. I used to love Tasha like a sister. But I couldn't' have her in my life. It was too much of a risk, and she simply wasn't worth putting Marcus and the baby in danger. "Tasha, I'm sorry you had to go through all that. I really am. But Marcus is going to be home soon. I think you should leave." I stood up, and headed for the door.

"He's a killer," she said, covering DeMarcus ears. "Do you hear me? He's a killer. I need your help."

I was speechless. I sat down, not knowing what to say. Of course, I wasn't surprised. I knew he killed his little brother. I knew he was capable of rape. He assaulted me enough times to know. I couldn't think about what my life would be like, if Marcus didn't find the med pack kept in kitchen cabinet. My baby wouldn't be here. The thought almost brought me to tears. Still, I felt strange having someone confirm my fears. Every time, I tried to talk to Marcus about it, he'd go on a tangent about how he could protect me. He was too busy trying to convince me not to worry. Instead of listening to what I said. The police weren't any help or comfort either. For awhile, I called Officer Moore everyday. Until, he got so tired of me calling, I could only reach his receptionist. Tasha knew more about the new Darius than I did. I was relieved to hear someone agreed with me. Darius was more than a threat. He was a cold blooded killer, capable of anything.

"Do you have proof?"

"Yeah. I have proof. The day I picked him up, I went through his pockets. I was trying to find out, if he was fucking somebody else, but came across something much worse. He had some middle aged white guys wallet in his pants. But that wasn't the worse part. He was carrying a picture of her." She unfolded a newspaper clipping of Emily Bronson. I remember reading an article about her online.

"Did you call the police? I asked, leaning off the edge of my chair.

"Hell nawl, I didn't go to the police. Darius would kill me next. He doesn't know that I'm here. I took a big risk coming to see you. He thinks I'm at work."

"How are you going to get away from him, if you don't involve the police?" I wasn't following her logic. Obviously, my pregnant behind couldn't beat him off her.

"I came to you, because your my sister. I need a place to stay." There was nothing but desperation in her eyes. Sadly, it didn't matter, because I couldn't help her. She made a fool out of me once. I wasn't going to let her doing it again.

"You know I can't do that."

"Fatima. I'm begging you. He's going to kill me, if you don't help. Please," she begged.

I walked to the door, and opened it. It may seem

cold, but I wasn't going to put my neck on the line for her. Especially not with a baby on the way. "It's time to go." She carried DeMarcus on her hip, and joined me at the door. I watched Marcus pull into the drive from the doorway.

"You're not going to help me? You know what he's capable of, and your just going to throw me out on the street. What about my baby? Are you really that selfish, Fatima?" True to form, her real self came out. She betrayed my trust, fucked my man, even though he wasn't shit, and now I'm supposed to feel bad because things went wrong.

"Hey. What's going on here?" Marcus looked confused to see Tasha and her baby.

"Nothing, honey. She was just leaving. I'll explain everything to you later." I said, pecking him on the cheek.

"You'll regret not helping me." she said, walking out the door, not knowing I already did.

Chapter 9

Marcus

Finally, I stopped trying, and accepted it was hopeless. Forcing my way into her heart wasn't getting me anywhere. So I decided to give up. She looked so pregnant, it pissed me off. Things weren't supposed to turn out this way. Looking at her swollen with my child made it impossible to ignore the distance between us. Our little princess would be here, any day now. The thought of her being born in such a toxic environment angered me more than anything. Materialistically, Fatima was prepared for birth. We purchased everything imaginable for a new baby and mom. The nursery was set, and ready to go. Fatima even had Shana come over to braid her hair. They only thing left on our to-do-list was getting married. But of course, that didn't go as planned. Instead of being happy, and excited to be with each other for the rest of our lives. We were sitting on my king sized bed throwing blows at each other.

Right before it was time to get in the car, she had to use the bathroom which wasn't bad. But then, five minutes pasted. Then ten. Then twenty. Before long, it was obvious she wasn't coming down. So I cut off the engine, and came back inside. She wasn't downstairs. So I checked the second floor. I found her crying and hyperventilating, like she was marrying a monster. Why be with me? If the thought of marrying me caused stress and anxiety? She claimed, she wasn't having a panic attack because of me. Supposedly, it was because of the night we got attacked. She could have been telling the truth. Unfortunately, I really didn't care. I had enough of the back and forth. Blaming crazy behavior on pregnancy hormones could only go so far.

"Fatima. I can't listen to this shit anymore. I thought we already went over this. We can't make decisions based on what, could happen? It's not practical, and it doesn't make any sense?" I'd been arguing with her for at least a half hour. We were supposed to be getting our marriage license. But suddenly, she got cold feet. I just didn't get it. If she loved me, and wanted to be my wife, what was the problem? Anytime, I tried to get close to her, she brought up my brother. I understood the night of the attack was awful. She would probably never heal from what happened. But seemed like it was becoming an unhealthy obsession. Scratch that, she had been obsessed for awhile.

"I know we have to move on. I want to be with you for the rest of my life. But that doesn't change the facts. He's out there, Marcus. I don't feel comfortable leaving the house, right now. I swear the other day, he was watching me when I went out with the girls. You have to believe me."

"Why the hell would he be watching you?" He's my brother. Remember? That night had nothing to do with you. He was coming after me. The motherfucker is crazy. I told you that. He already killed my brother. He damn near killed my mom. The psychopath probably wanted to take me out, because my dad didn't leave him shit." Her naivety was really started to piss me off. I tried to be patient with her. Especially since she was pregnant. But our little girl was going to be here soon, and I wanted us to be married before she arrived.

"Do you really want to get married like this?"

"Married like what, Fatima? I'm tired of the excuses. Just come out, and say it. You don't love me, and you never have. Anytime I try to get you to be open, and honest, you shut down. And to make matters worse, you walk around like I'm too stupid to notice. I'm tired of trying. It's too exhausting. If you don't want to make this work, we don't have too. I'm out of here.

"Marcus. Wait. Where are you going?" she begged.

"Does it even matter? You don't need me here. You can't like I'm a bitch. You don't believe I can protect you. I might as well be that coat rack sitting in the corner. You have the same amount of faith in my ability to protect you. Besides, when we are together, all you talk about is that night. You don't ask about me, my job, or anything else. You're obsessed with my brother. You can't see past him." She looked like she wanted to say something like usual, but didn't. Why couldn't she just be honest, and tell me what was on her mind.

"You're right. I haven't been fair to you. I just don't know how to get over what happened." I walked around the bed. Sat beside her, then wrapped my arm around her shoulder.

"We can get through this, babe. But you have to open up. When you talk to me, it seems like your holding something back. What is it? Whatever you're going through. We can get through it together." She moved away from me, and leaned up against the headboard.

"Do you promise to stick by my side, no matter what?"

I took a deep breath, and nodded yes.

"We didn't meet organically. We were setup."

I scrunched up my face. What she said didn't make any sense. The first time we met was at my office. She brought DeMarcus in for his appointment. I remembered like it was yesterday. She asked me out, but I turned her down. I didn't think I was ready to get back in the game. She said, her friend Tasha couldn't make it, because she had to go to work. How could that have been a setup? "What do you mean? We met at my office. That wasn't a setup." I said, rubbing the top of my head.

One tear rolled down her cheek, but she quickly wiped it away. "Remember what you said okay?"

"I remember. Just tell me what you've been holding back."

"Tasha wasn't at work. She wanted me to meet you that day."

I let out a nervous laugh, and threw my hands up. "Stop playing girl. You almost gave me a heart attack. So you wanted to meet a doctor. That's not a big deal. You, and every other woman, wants to snag a doctor. That's practically the dream of every single woman."

"Let me get this out. That's not all." She must have been holding on to some serious stuff. Another tear fell, and she swept it away. "DeMarcus is your nephew. His last name is Stewart, because Darius didn't want me to find out he got Tasha pregnant."

"What are you talking about? That boy isn't my family. How would you know if he was, anyway?" Slowly I pieced together the puzzle. "He didn't want you to find out, Tasha was pregnant. You were sleeping with my brother?" She couldn't have meant what she said. All of a sudden, I felt like I was swimming in air. There had to be something I missed.

"I'm sorry, baby. I didn't know how to tell you." Her cheeks were covered in streams.

I was so shocked, I couldn't react. I waited so long to hear the truth, I begged her to put everything on the table. Now I wished, she could take it all back. I scooted to edge of the bed, and crossed my arms. "What else?" I asked, raising my chin.

"Marcus, I'm sorry."

"Shoot."

"I met Darius, four years before we met. I thought I was in love."

I jumped off the bed, I couldn't help myself. How the fuck could she say, she loved him. He was always a monster. He'd been that way since we were kids. Apparently I didn't know her at all. "You loved him. You loved him." Tears were flowing from my eyes now.

"I didn't want to hurt you, Marcus." I could barely understand, over her sobs. "I love you so much. I want us to be together. I didn't know how to tell you. Our relationship wasn't part of the plan.

"The plan! You had a fucking plan. This shit really was a setup." I was screaming now. I felt like my world was crashing down. I thought I loved this woman, when I didn't' even know her.

"It wasn't my plan. It was all Darius. If I didn't to go through with it," she paused. "He forced me. I didn't have a choice."

"He forced you. The thought of being with me was so bad, he had to force you." Every time she opened her mouth, it only got worse.

"No. It's not like that. He was getting blackmailed, and needed half of your inheritance to stay out of jail. He thought, I could talk you out of it."

Fuck. She was supposed to be having my child soon. Now all of this is coming out. Where could we go from here? No wonder she was acting funny. She brought misery back into my life. I went against my instincts, and accepted her advances, now I'm in this fucked up situation.

"Marcus please." She wailed, and grabbed at my shoulder. She tried to lean against me, but I walked away. "If I didn't do what he said, he'd rape me again. I had no other choice, Marcus. Don't do this. I love you."

Suddenly it hit me. "Is Briana even mine?" I asked, tearing my eyes through her. All this time, she watched as I jumped up and down like an idiot. She knew damn well the baby probably wasn't mine. I couldn't believe it. I probably should have been more considered about the rape, but I couldn't care. It was impossible. She ripped my heart apart like it was piece of rib eye steak. I lost all self control. The two good things I had to look forward to were gone. Briana may not be mine. And it didn't look like we were getting married, anymore. I couldn't stay, and listen to anymore of what she had to say. The room was filled with tears, anyway. Fatima was crying so hard, she couldn't speak. I took her silence as my answer. God how could this happen? My baby girl wasn't even mine? I waited months for this day. I even reminisced about how happy I was when I married Allison, and had Jamie. My experience with Fatima wasn't similar in anyway. The whole scenario smelled like shit. I thought we'd be celebrating our new union, and commitment to each other right now. Instead, I couldn't wait to get away from her. I grabbed my keys, and jumped in the car. I was ready to drown my sorrows.

Chapter 10

Fatima

I couldn't breath. My heart felt like it was literally breaking. Every part of my body was rattled with stress. I sucked in air, as best I could. But, I couldn't stop hyperventilating. The worst case scenario just played out in front of my eyes, just like I expected. I didn't want to tell him the truth, but the weight of the lies was eating me up. They were getting harder, and harder, to hold onto. The fact, he kept accusing me of not loving him, because I was distant, made it impossible to continue living a lie.

Marcus left about an hour. The entire time he was gone, I regretted not getting in the car. I did want to marry him. I still wanted to, but the thought of leaving the house, sent me into a downward spiral. I tried to explain why I couldn't go to the courthouse. I knew Darius was out there waiting for an opportunity to strike. There was no denying he was still following me. I didn't have any proof. Besides, the tiny hairs raised on the back of my neck, whenever I decided to leave home. I only left twice, since that night. Once to clear out my apartment. Once to buy baby clothes with my girls, and both times he was there waiting in the thick. It was true. I couldn't prove it was him, who set off my car alarm. But who else could it be? Marcus was at work. And I was with the only other people I dealt with, at the time. I had no doubt in my mind. It was him. Nothing could convince me it wasn't. Of course, I went to my monthly prenatal appointments, too. But other than that, I stayed at home.

Why was Marcus so old fashioned? It shouldn't have mattered, if we got married after Darius was arrested or dead. I wanted to marry him without fear, or worry, looming in the back of my mind. Doing it before then, would cast a negative shadow over our union. I didn't want that. When Briana got older, she wouldn't care, or know the difference, anyway. I couldn't help remembering the hurtful things he said before leaving. Of course, I understood he was angry, and that it would take time for him to process everything I said. Still, it hurt to hear him say he didn't want to be with me anymore.

Briana was kicking, and flipping around the entire time we were arguing. I ignored her increased activity, and tried to stay focus on the conversation at hand. I didn't need him excusing me of avoiding him again. Plus, once I got started, I couldn't stop. Saying it once was bad enough, I figured blurting everything out at once was the best way to go, because I couldn't do it any other way. Now that he was gone, I noticed she wasn't letting up. I placed my hand on my stomach, and realized it was hard as a rock. Should I call Marcus, or head to the hospital alone?

AAH!

The pain was getting stronger. I paced back and forth, trying to walk it off. I didn't want to go in, if it was a false alarm. I read stress could cause contractions, but it usually was a sign of false labor, and not the real deal.

"Ooh, aah, ooh, aah!" It was only getting worse. I reached for the side of my dresser, but missed. Everything on top of it, went crashing onto the floor. Luckily, I fell against the wall, instead of on my back. I needed him to get back home, asap. I dialed his number, but it went straight to voice mail which never happened. I dialed again. Still no response. Obviously, he was still pissed. I jotted down a quick note in case he came back home. Left with no other option, I grabbed my purse and labor bag, before heading for the door. My little girl was coming home sooner than I thought. It didn't matter if I was prepared, or not.

The trip to the hospital was insane. I kept swerving in and out of traffic on the way over. It was a miracle I got there in one piece, and didn't get pulled over. I shut off the engine, in front of labor and delivery, and gripped the steering wheel tightly. I was having the contraction of my life. I heard and felt a strong pop. Before I knew it, the seat of my pants and car were soaked with clear fluid. Dammit. My water broke. I stepped outside with my labor bag and purse thrown over my shoulder. Another contraction was coming on strong. I leaned on the hood of my car, and bared down. She wasn't going to wait for much longer. I grunted into the black sky, and prayed for the strength to make it inside. God. I needed Marcus right now.

"Sorry, girl. I tried to warn you." A voice said from behind me. I felt a prick on the side of my neck, and was out.

*****

The sound of the hood bouncing up and down was excruciating. I reached up, and covered my ears. At the same time, I could feel brightness shining on my face as I slowly opened my eyes. Doing so irritated the sharp pain already cutting through the top of my head. I saw a chain tied from the hood to the latch. It was preventing the trunk from opening or swinging closed. Disgusted by the smell of exhaust fumes, I gagged. Slowly, I gathered my senses. It was still dark outside. It wasn't the sun shining in my face. It was headlights, from the cars in front of me. What happened? Was the first thought to enter my mind. The last thing I remembered was my water breaking. Instinctively, I reached for my belly. Then, I let out a huge sigh of relief. Thank god. She was still there, and moving.

"Aah!"

There went another contraction. I couldn't do anything to relieve the pain. Scrunched inside the back of the trunk, I wasn't able to stretch out, or comfort myself. Hopeless. I began to cry.

"Ssh" I heard someone say from inside the vehicle. "I think she's awake."

I covered my mouth, and did my best to listen. The car went silent, but kept moving. I crossed my fingers, and prayed to god it wouldn't stop.

"I did exactly what you said. Why are you mad?" a female voice asked. I was pretty sure it was Tasha. I would know her voice anywhere.

"I'm mad because I don't need you questioning me shit." Darius said, confirming my worst fear.

"I'm not, baby. As a woman, I know a little bit about these things. I was just making a suggestion."

"A suggestion, huh. Nobody is going to make me miss the birth of my child. Not you, Fatima, Marcus, or any other muthafucker. That's my right as father."

"That's right, baby. I totally agree. I just thought,

we should wait until after she gave birth to kidnap her."

"Bitch are you dumb? I'm not waiting on shit. I deserve to be there, when my daughter enters the world, like I said."

"You're right. Don't let me ruin your moment. I'm so stupid. What I said, didn't make any sense. I don't know what I was thinking."

"And what did I tell you about thinking? I don't keep your ass around to think. All I need you to do, is what I said. You dig? I can do most things with one hand. But other shit, I need your help with. If things get messy tonight. I may need you to jump in."

"What do you mean, you're keeping me around in case things get messy? I don't plan on going no where." Tasha said with an attitude.

"Fatima don't have a lot of kids, like your trifling ass. She may need help delivering the baby. If she does, you may have to jump in." There was no way he was coming near me. I'd be damned, if he touched my baby. I started feeling around the trunk as best I could. I needed to find something to defend myself.

"You want me to help you deliver a baby. Oh hell nawl. I didn't sign up for this shit. Where are we going to do this at? You need a sterile environment to have baby. I've had enough to know. Like you so kindly pointed out."

"Shut the fuck up, bitch. I'm trying to drive. If you don't be quiet. I'll put your ass in the trunk. Like a told you before, I know what I'm doing. I have the perfect spot, picked out. There's only a few miles left, before we get there. We're going to deliver at this abandoned veterinarian center. I ordered scrubs, sterilizer, scissors, and a scalpel. I even bought a clamp to cut the cord. I got this shit, all figured out, I'm telling you. I read Emergency Childbirth from cover to cover. So there ain't shit to worry about."

"Whatever you say. But childbirth don't work like that."

"The more you talk, the more I think I made a mistake. Maybe I don't need to keep your ass around."

"Why do you keep saying that? I don't plan on going no where. You make it sound like you plan on taking me out, or something."

Darius laughed, and a chill shot up my spin. I was crying so hard with my hand over my mouth, it felt like I was having convulsions.

"Did I stutter, bitch. Yeah, I said it. I'm keeping you around. If you keep talking though, I may change my mind. What the fuck are you going to do about it, anyway, bitch."

The car jerked roughly to the side. My head banged against the front of the trunk, not expecting it. Blood dripped over my eye, as the car jumped in and out of lanes. We were no longer on city streets. He turned onto a dirt road, and traveled a few miles, before parking into a forest of trees.

"I told you bitch, I told you." Darius was in a rage. I could hear him banging on the dashboard over Tasha's cries. Out of no where, things got quiet. The door opened, then closed. I could hear him panting, and pacing back and forth in front of the trunk. He walked out of my eye sight, and returned to the car. The next thing I saw was him dragging Tasha body. With a machete as long as my arm. He chopped her up, bit by bit, in front of me. She wasn't my friend, sister, or enemy, anymore. The only thing left was a pile of mangled body parts.

Darius looked between the slit in the trunk. His face was covered in blood, and crazed. I howled so loud, I scared the baby. We both jumped in horror. He fiddled with the padlock, removed the chain, and opened the trunk.

"Hey, Fatty. It's been too long." He wiped the blood off my face with the back of his hand, and dropped her body parts all around me. "It won't be much longer, baby. We're almost there." He kissed me, and replaced the chain.

"No … please no." I whimpered. He got back in the car, and started driving again.

Her corpse was warm, wet, and all over my body. I couldn't take it, anymore. My mind collapsed. I howled and screamed, as loud as I could. What the fuck was I going to do? Somewhere along the way, the contractions stopped, but I felt no relief. They were replaced with a pain too great to describe. I couldn't hope or pray. Reality set in. There would be no rescue team. No one knew I was gone, let alone missing. If they did, it wouldn't matter, because I was kidnapped by a ghost.

Chapter 11

"Here's a drink from the lady in the corner." The bartender said, pointing to a woman scantly dressed.

There was no doubting her intentions. Ten of her twenty dollar jeans were in her crotch. And the shirt she wore only covered half her breasts. The rest was on full display. From what I could see, she wasn't my type. Most men would probably find her attractive. But, she was too basic for me. A woman like her was a dime a dozen in the hood, which was one of the many reasons I didn't live there. She was short, thick, and wore a long weave down her back, which wasn't too bad to look at. It obviously wasn't her hair, though. There definitely was an Asian woman running around somewhere bald-headed. I preferred natural beauties. I didn't care for a lot of makeup, and extra shit. Regardless. I nodded my appreciation, and downed the drink. There was no reason to let a good shot go to waste. Especially, when it was what I needed most.

She smiled back, and made her way over. I flagged down the bartender, and motioned for a refill. I was already drunk, but apparently not drunk enough, I really didn't want to talk to her, or anybody else for that matter. Fatima had been running through my mind all night. She called a couple of times earlier, but I turned my phone off, sending her calls straight to voice mail. I hated doing it. But I didn't want to rehash our conversation.

The things she said really fucked me up. I needed to fog up my mind, before I could deal with the situation at home. I had no problem admitting I wasn't man enough to handle what she said. The thought of her with him, made me sick. Rape was one thing. I didn't like that it happened. It was horrible. She shouldn't have been put through that. No one should endure that type of pain. But at least, I could rest easy knowing, she only had feelings for me. Now I knew, she used to love him. The same way, she claims to love me, now.

I just couldn't trust a word she says. What type of woman didn't know who the father of her child is? Yeah. She claimed, he raped her around the time Briana was conceived. But how could I know that was true? She lied to me for over a year, and I didn't even know about it. What other secrets were hiding in the closest? I should have never fell for her. I could kick myself for being so stupid. My instincts told me to keep my head down. Until I was ready to jump back in the dating pool. Now, I was more in love than ever, to a woman that could be pregnant by my psychotic brother.

"Would you like some company, handsome?" She interrupted my thoughts, and slid onto the bar stool next to me.

I tipped my shot glass at her, and downed another shot. "Sure. It's a free country." I said, rubbing my temples with one hand.

"Woman problems?" she grinned, flashing her dimples.

"How'd you guess? I must look pretty pathetic, huh. It didn't take you long to put that together."

"Don't be silly. You don't look pathetic at all. In fact, you're actually kinda cute." She looked a lot better close up. Maybe I rushed to judgment.

I whistled, and motioned for the bartender to fill her up. I might as well enjoy some good conversation while I was here. "Go ahead, and put it on my tab."

"Thanks."

"No problem. It's been awhile since I got a compliment." I said, bitterly.

"Well. I'll have to do something about that. A handsome man like yourself, should never feel unappreciated it. Your wife is a brave woman to let you go out alone." She was laying it on thick. But I didn't care. I needed my ego, and other things stroked.

"What's your name again?" I asked, licking my lips while sneaking a peak of the tightly wrapped mounds spilling out of her shirt. They definitely looked good enough to eat.

"My name is Carla."

"Nice to meet you Carla. I'm Marcus."

"Do you like what you see, Marcus?" She stood up, and pressed her chest against me. "All this could be yours, if you want it to be."

I swallowed the thick lump that formed in my throat. Finally my luck was turning around. "Yeah. You're looking real good tonight, Carla." It had been so long since I busted a nut. I was practically dragging my balls behind me. I wanted to get some pussy so bad, I almost didn't care where it came from.

"Good. Because I like what I see too. Do you mind if I give it a try?"

I nodded my head like a toddler anticipating a cookie. I didn't know what she was going to do next, and I didn't care. My nose was wide open. I wanted to do, whatever she wanted. I just needed some relief.

"Come here, baby." She said, reaching her hands into the front of my pants. I ain't gonna lie. I squealed like a little bitch. The shit was feeling so good. I forgot I was in public.

"My, my, my. Look at you. You're big boy. Aren't you?" I grinned with pride. It was about time, I got some acknowledgment for my gifts. She slipped her warm tongue in my mouth, and began stroking me up and down like a pro. "Do you like that, baby?"

I nodded in pleasure, and she continued.

"I can give you anything you want. What can you give me?" She whispered in my ear. Suddenly, she removed her hand. Zipped up my pants, discreetly. And sat back down on her stool.

My mind was swimming. I didn't want her to stop. Things were just starting to get good.

"I can take care of you. Can you take care of me?" She asked, seductively sucking on the length of her straw.

I realized, what she was asking. She wasn't looking for a casual encounter. There were dollars signs in her eyes. She wanted to get paid. "How much?" I asked, taking another shot. I was mad, hurt, and horny. I'd pay anything for some relief.

"How much am I worth to you baby?" She leaned back in the stool, and started rubbing herself. The bar was so crowded, no one noticed.

"Five hundred dollars." I said proudly, throwing the cash on the bar.

She put the money in between her breast, and cooed. "Thank you, daddy. Give me one more, and I'll meet you in the bathroom." She strutted across the room with my money in hand.

I quickly paid the tab, and followed her into the men's bathroom. She locked the door behind me, and pulled off her shirt. She had the most perfect breasts I'd ever seen. I reached for them, but she pulled back.

"One more, remember?" she said, removing her pants and underwear.

I dug into my wallet, and paid her fee. I was just happy to be getting some pussy. She shoved her breast in my face. And I filled my mouth with both nipples. I was licking and sucking like a starved beast. It was amazing to hold a woman again. It had been so long, I felt like a born again virgin. She dropped to her knees and took me in her mouth. She was working me from nut to tip. There wasn't a surface she didn't cover. The shit was feeling so good, I shuttered, and nearly exploded. She pulled me out of her mouth, and bent over. I slid inside, and started fucking her from behind. I hate to admit, but I came almost immediately. It felt like the best thirty seconds of my life.

"Thanks," she said, while washing off in the sink. She put her clothes on, and kissed me goodbye.

I looked down at my dick like it committed a crime. Thanks? She couldn't have said, what I think she said. Could she? Immediately, I sobered up. And it hit. I just had sex with a prostitute in a disgusting public bathroom. What the fuck was wrong with me? I'm supposed to be a doctor, I thought to myself. After she left, I washed up too, and put on my clothes. I needed to get back to my baby. Asap.

When I turned on my phone. I saw I had ten missed calls. Fuck. There had to be something wrong. Fatima never blew my phone up. Guilt suddenly overwhelmed me. What if something was wrong with her, or the baby. I was so angry at myself. I abandoned my responsibilities at home. I had to make it up to her. I grabbed my shit, and jetted towards the house. I kept calling on the way over, but she wasn't picking up the phone. When I got home, I looked for her inside, but she wasn't there. Something was definitely wrong. I did find a note on the refrigerator though. It read:

I'm at the hospital. I couldn't wait any longer.

Love Fatima

I hit the refrigerator so hard. A dent the size of my fist was in it. I really fucked up this time. I couldn't let her have the baby without me. I called labor and delivery to get her room number. To my surprise, they said she wasn't there. How the fuck was that possible? She couldn't have just disappeared. Our wedding rings sat on the counter, and told the full story. She was right. Darius wasn't going to let her go. I should have none better than to leave her alone. That motherfucker had my baby.

Chapter 12

Darius

I'd been waiting for this moment for over nine months. We were finally back together, at last. I was so excited to have Fatima with me again. It was hard keeping my shit together. Of course, everything didn't go as planned. I had to ax that bitch Tasha, before I wanted to. Still, I couldn't regret keeping her around. Since, making her the beneficiary of my life insurance policy was the only way I could afford to make this shit happen. She was so smoked out, and out of her mind, she didn't even realize what she was signing. When I passed her the paperwork. Little did she know, she was the lucky owner of this establishment, a warehouse in the city, and a bank account with five hundred G's in it. I even had her sign a will, making my son the sole beneficiary and trustee, if she died. I couldn't help smiling proudly to myself. My plan was finally coming together.

I hated making Fatima ride in the trunk. I knew that shit had to be uncomfortable as fuck. But what other choice did I have? I couldn't risk her drawing any attention from other drivers on the road. Plus, Tasha fucked up. Since she didn't give her enough morphine to keep her asleep. I told her stupid ass to double the dose. Fatima wasn't supposed to be wake up until we reached our destination. I pulled off the dirt road, and into the abandoned animal clinic parking lot, right outside the city. The large amount of abandoned buildings in Oklahoma, was one of the few things I liked about living here. It made it easy for a rolling stone like me.

Fatima stopped screaming about a half hour ago. I took that as I sign, she was asleep. After the long night she had, I'm sure she needed it. I cut off the engine, and decided to take advantage of the situation by double checking her room, before bringing her in. I wanted to make sure everything was perfect for her, and my baby. I hopped out the car, and ran inside.

Swinging the door open, I was relieved to see everything was just how I left it. The lobby was empty, except for a few old chairs lining the wall. I jogged to the back of the clinic, and scoped out the operating room. The space was updated, and nice. I really did a good job. I bought one of those fancy beds, you can change the settings on. If she got uncomfortable, I could raise or drop the bed with a push of a button. I even had a bassinet set up, right next to the bed, the baby. I couldn't get my hands on one of those expensive machines that monitored blood pressure, and shit. I figured I wouldn't need it anyway. Since back in the day, all they needed was a hot pot of water, some towels, and maybe a piece of wood to bite on. As far as I could tell, I was ahead of the game. She'd be alright. I bet there's a woman giving birth somewhere in the bush right now. Besides, the room was well equipped. There was a sink and left over supplies from when the clinic was open. If her contractions did get too bad, or something went wrong, I had a stack of medications only a few feet away. Given they were for animals.

"She's getting away!" a voice screamed from inside my head. "He's slipping. What the fuck is he waiting for? Your wasting your time trying to help him out." another voice argued. "He's gonna mess this shit up. Right at the end," a third voice interjected.

I slapped the sides of my head, and yelled, "Shut up." I hated when they started saying shit like that. I wasn't slipping. Everything was going according to plan. Except for a few minor details. I pulled the glass dick out of my pocket, and started sucking away. I needed to relax my mind a little bit. My lungs lit up, and my shoulders dropped, before I exhaled deeply. The voices turned down, and started talking quietly amongst themselves. I let out a huge sigh of relief, rolled my neck, and went outside to get Fatima.

"Please … please … Darius. Just let me go. I promise not to say anything," she begged.

I ignored her, and started putting Tasha's feet into a black plastic bag. I needed to do something with the body, before I dealt with Fatima. She started screaming again. So I closed the trunk. I didn't need any distractions. There had to be away to get rid of it. I surveyed the grounds, and spotted a metal garbage can behind the building. I'd have to put it in there. I bagged up the rest, and dumped it in the trash can, but I still had another problem. I didn't have any lighter fluid or fuel. Lucky for me, there was plenty of twigs and sticks laying on the ground. "I'd just have to make do," I said out loud to myself. I stirred up the pieces with wood I found laying around, then lit the bin on fire. I knew there was no chance of getting caught, we were miles away from town. I took a few moments, and savored the smell, before bringing Fatima inside her suit.

She was lifeless, her body was limp and stained by blood, carrying her through the threshold was a challenge, but I managed to place her softly on the bed. I brushed away hair covering her eye, and kissed her deeply. Her eyes were a little low, and a bit foggy. But other than that, our kiss was the way I pictured it, in my mind. She didn't resist or even try to fight me. She just laid still on the bed with her eyes closed. I pressed my finger under her noise, and waited. I was relieved to find she was still breathing.

I watched as her stomach faintly raised up and down. I couldn't imagine my life without her. I needed Fatima. I didn't want her. She was the only person who truly knew me. When I looked into her eyes I didn't judgment, dollar signs, or game. I saw love and genuine concern. I needed to see that again. I knew kidnapping her wouldn't work. I had to restore her faith in me, and our relationship. It used to be the only thing she wanted was for us to be a family. I was ready to give her that now. Supporting her during the delivery of our child was the best way I could prove, I changed for the better.

Fatima clutched her stomach, and screamed. "Help. Somebody. Help."

A grabbed her hand, and wiped her forehead with a damp wash cloth I prepared. "Just breathe baby. It's going to be okay. I got everything under control."

"Aah! Aah! I can't take it." She was flailing her hands, and sobbing. "Get off of me. I need a doctor." She wailed, but I knew she didn't mean it.

"Tell me what you need baby. I got everything set." She ignored me, but started pulling at her pants. "Don't worry. I got you." I pulled them, and her panties off. She reached between her legs, and screamed.

"She's ripping me. I can't take it. Oh god. Help me. Help me." When she pulled her hand up, it was covered in blood. I looked between her legs, but didn't know what I was seeing.

"What do you want me to do?" I ran to the medicine cabinet looking for drugs. There had to be something to dull the pain.

"Take me back. Darius. You have to take me back. She's going to die, if you don't."

"I got it." I ran over and tried to stick her with a shot of buprenophine. It was typically used for cats, but I figured, it knocked her out during the drive over. It should definitely take the edge off of the pain.

She slapped the syringe out of my hand. And grabbed at the sides of the rail. "Oh my baby. She's not moving. You killed her. You son of a bitch!" Her mouth was seething with hate. Fatima never yelled, or spoke to me like that. I could feel the rage coming off her.

"Babe, you don't mean that. Calm down. I know you're in a lot of pain."

I couldn't tell if she was laughing or crying. It sounded like she was doing both. "I'm not your fucking babe. You're a psychopath. Why couldn't you just leave us alone?"

"Did you hear that?" a voice snicked from inside. "I did. She called him crazy like everybody else. I told him she wasn't no different." I ripped the medicine cabinet down. They didn't know her like I did. I paced back and forth, trying to calm down.

"I'm sorry, Darius. I didn't mean it." She was reaching between her legs again. "I need your help okay."

I couldn't tell if she was being honest or lying. I wasn't in the mood for games. "You called me a son of bitch. Are you crazy. Don't you ever talk to me like that again." I was heated. I loved Fatima, but she wasn't going to disrespect me. I'd be damned, if she talked to me like I was a bitch.

"Just help me get her out. We don't have time to waste. I can't lose my baby."

"We have to work on our communication skills. If were going to make this work. How are we going to raise a healthy daughter, if there's so much bad blood between us?"

Fatima started laughing or crying again. I couldn't tell which one. Apparently, she still thought I was playing. I'd take care of that shit real quick.

"What are you doing?" she asked rolling from side to side.

I wasn't going to dignify her ass with a response. I picked up the bottle of buprenophine, and three large syringes off the floor. I filled them all up, and jumped on top of her. This bitch was treating me like everybody else. Before she could respond. I stuck all three in her neck, and pushed. She was out like a light. Finally, I could get down to business.

I'm not gonna lie. I was more than disappointed, she hadn't come to her sense yet. I was really hoping to become a family man. But apparently, she needed a little more motivation than I thought. I slapped on a pair of latex gloves, put on my green scrubs, and cleaned the surface of her belly with some damp washed clothes. I watched plenty of episodes of a Baby Story. I knew what I was doing. C-sections looked pretty simple to me. The medical field was just trying to monopolize the market.

First, I wiped across her panty line with some alcohol preps. Then, I made a clean cut from hip to hip. She flinched, and her eyes moved, but she didn't wake up. I put my hands between the cut, and pulled. Blood splattered across my face. Immediately, she howled, and setup in bed. I think she was in shock, because she fell back down just as quick. I pulled my baby out by her butt, and flipped her over. She was stuck. There was no other way to get her out. Delivery was even easier than I expected. She was blue, quiet, and slimy all over. I knew she was supposed to be crying. I laid her across the fold of my arm, and patted her back with my only hand. Mucus came flying out her mouth, and she began to cry.

"We did it, babe. We did it." Fatima was

knocked out, and couldn't here me. I kissed her forehead anyway, and started cleaning off my beautiful daughter with a towel. "It was a long road getting you here, but you finally made it." I kissed my daughter on the cheek, and called Marcus. I was eager to share the good news.

"Fatima?" His voice was hoarse like he'd been crying. I always knew my brother was a bitch.

"Nawl, this ain't Fatima, nigga. You should really get over here, soon though. She's bleeding out. I don't know how long she'll last. But my baby girl is doing excellent."

"I'll kill you motherfucker!"

I hung up the phone, before he could finish his threat. That bitch wasn't about to do shit. I sent the clinic address to his cell phone. He needed to get here soon, if we our little game was going to continue. I smiled to myself, knowing I gave Fatima all the motivation she would need to come back home.